For Diana Cockerton
JD

For Lisa
CT

First U.S. edition 1995

Library of Congress Catalog Card Number 94-74045

ISBN 1-56402-551-9

2 4 6 8 10 9 7 5 3 1

Printed in Hong Kong

The pictures in this book were done in watercolor and ink.

Candlewick Press
2067 Massachusetts Avenue
Cambridge, Massachusetts 02140

OOPS-A-DAISY!
· AND OTHER TALES FOR TODDLERS ·

Joyce Dunbar *illustrated by* Carol Thompson

CANDLEWICK PRESS
CAMBRIDGE, MASSACHUSETTS

OOPS-A-DAISY!

Sadie came to play.

"I can be
upside down,"
said Sadie.

"So can I," I said.

"I can go head over heels," said Sadie.

 "So can I," I said.

"I can wear my pants inside out," said Sadie.

"So can I," I said.

"I can put my
sweater on backwards,"
said Sadie.
"So can I," I said.

"Let's be back to back,"
said Sadie.
And we were.

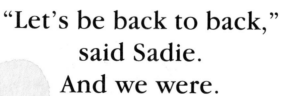

"Let's be
higgledy-piggledy,"
said Sadie.
    And we were.

"Let's go oops-a-daisy," said Sadie. And we did.
Sadie bumped her head on mine. I bumped
my head on Sadie's.

"Ooow!" Sadie yowled.   "Ouch!" I howled.

"That was a lot of fun, wasn't it?" said Sadie.
"Let's play it again," I said.

WHAT IF?

I went into the yard
with Grump.
We played "What if?"

"What if I sneezed,"
I said to Grump,
"and all the worms came
up and sneezed too?"

"That would be funny,"
said Grump.

"What if I danced," I said to Grump, "and all the mice came out and danced with me?"

"That would be funny," said Grump.

"What if I whistled," I said,
"and all the birds flew down
and whistled too?"

"You can't whistle,"
said Grump.

"I know I can't," I said.
"But I'll be able to whistle
one day . . . and then
you never know
what might
happen."

NICKY COMES TO PLAY

"Nicky's coming to play today,"
said Mom. "Do you want
Nicky to come and play?"
"Yes," I said, "I do."

Nicky was shy when
he came.
He wouldn't
look.

I showed Nicky my toy truck. Then he looked.
Nicky wanted to play with my toy truck.
I gave it to him. He drove
it over the sofa.

I wanted the toy truck too.
I took it from him and gave him
my play dough machine.

Nicky made squiggly
things with the play
dough machine.

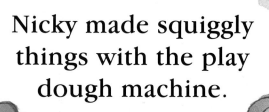

I wanted the play dough machine. I took it from him and gave him Grump to play with.

Nicky cuddled Grump. Grump's mine to cuddle.

I took Grump away from Nicky.
Nicky cried.

After that he went home. Now I had all
my toys to myself. I had my toy truck and
my play dough machine and Grump.

They didn't seem as much fun anymore,
so I went off and sucked my blanket.

I hope Nicky comes again soon.

THE BEST-DRESSED TEDDY

"They're having a competition at the fair this year," said Mom. "Look, it's for the best-dressed teddy bear."

"Grump doesn't wear dresses," I said.
"You're right," said Mom. "So let's
make him some pants instead."

She made him some polka-dotted pants

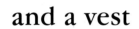 and a vest

and some shoes.

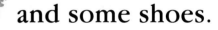

I made him a hat.

He didn't look like Grump anymore.
He looked like some other bear.

We took him to the fair. There were hundreds of teddy bears, all dressed up. The judge looked at them all.

"You're looking very spiffy today," he said to Grump.
Grump just looked Grumpy.

He didn't win.
A bear in a sailor suit won.

I took Grump home.
I took off all his new clothes.
"You should have gone
without any clothes,"
I said, "then you
would have won."